Behind the Wheel of a
MONSTER TRUCK

BY ALEX MONNIG

Published by The Child's World®
1980 Lookout Drive • Mankato, MN 56003-1705
800-599-READ • www.childsworld.com

Acknowledgments
The Child's World®: Mary Berendes, Publishing Director
Red Line Editorial: Design, editorial direction, and production
Photographs ©: Manu Fernandez/AP Images, cover, 1; Evren Kalinbacak/Shutterstock Images, 4, 18; Shutterstock Images, 6; Juan Carlos Ulate/Reuters/Corbis, 8; Royalbroil CC3.0, 11; Jim Damaske/ZumaPress/Newscom, 12; Barry Salmons/Shutterstock Images, 14; Bizuayehu Tesfaye/AP Images, 17, 20

Copyright © 2016 by The Child's World®
All rights reserved. No part of this book may be reproduced or utilized in any form or by any means without written permission from the publisher.

ISBN 9781634074308

LCCN 2015946341

Printed in the United States of America
PA02353

Table of CONTENTS

Chapter 1
SHOWTIME SWEAT 5

Chapter 2
THE MEANING
BEHIND THE MONSTERS 9

Chapter 3
PUTTING IN TIME 13

Chapter 4
GO TIME 19

Glossary 22
To Learn More 23
Selected Bibliography 23
Index 24
About the Author 24

Chapter 1

SHOWTIME SWEAT

You are sweating. Your helmet is sitting snugly on your head. Your black and bright green gloves are covering your hands, which are wrapped tightly around the steering wheel. You are in control of a monster truck.

The monster truck is also black and bright green. Its name, Destructor, is written in glossy green letters on the side. On the front hood are two squinting green eyes. Destructor weighs about 10,000 pounds (4,536 kg). That is about twice as heavy as the pickup truck your dad drives to work each day. And Destructor's tires are nearly as tall as he is. Each one weighs about 800 pounds (363 kg).

Monster truck events take place in giant arenas across the country. Tonight, you are in a stadium that also hosts football games. More than 50,000 people are here. The lights are bright.

◀ **Monster trucks' huge tires allow them to do tricks and roll over objects.**

Their white beams cover the track. The other trucks are already lined up.

Destructor shines in the light. It is squeaky-clean. But it will not be that way for long. It is almost time for your first official run as a professional monster truck driver.

The crowd starts to cheer. Your helmet covers your ears, and the engine of the monster truck is loud. But you can still hear the yelling and clapping fans. Your family members are in the arena. They and thousands of others are getting excited.

A few of your friends are also in the stadium. They know how much time you have put into getting ready for the event.

You are excited to show your family and friends what you have been working so hard on. You are excited for the chance to compete. You are also excited to impress the crowd. But you have to concentrate. It's showtime.

◂ **Monster trucks may start out clean and shiny. But they often leave events dinged and dirty.**

Chapter 2

THE MEANING BEHIND THE MONSTERS

You remember first seeing monster trucks on TV. You were amazed at the giant vehicles. They looked like they belonged in comic books. How could these machines be real? You had to learn more. So you borrowed books from the library to get more information.

You learned monster trucks became popular in the 1970s. They grew bigger and better over the years. The Monster Truck Racing Association created rules for races.

Monster trucks need to weigh at least 9,000 pounds (4,082 kg). The minimum weight requirement is for safety. If the trucks are too light, they might flip over easily during tight turns and jumps. Tires are supposed to be 5.5 feet (1.7 m) tall. This also is for safety

◂ **Monster trucks can crush cars and buses.**

reasons. Keeping all the tires the same size means no truck can sacrifice safety for performance.

You remember seeing a monster truck in person for the first time when you were five. The Crusher was in town. Your parents took you to see it.

You could not believe how massive it was. You could not touch the top of the tires, even when you jumped. You had to use a ladder to climb into the **cab**. That was where the driver would sit.

The monster truck's cab was more open than normal vehicles. The floor was made of silver metal. There were some gauges with dials on the right-hand side. But there was not a normal **dashboard**. There was no backseat, either.

EARLY MONSTER

Bigfoot is the oldest monster truck. Bob Chandler created it in 1975 in St. Louis, Missouri. He kept wrecking his regular truck. So he kept rebuilding it bigger each time. It became huge. Bigfoot was one of the first monsters that crushed other cars. Chandler first crushed a car in 1981. Since then, people have built more than 20 versions of Bigfoot.

The Crusher did not need that stuff. Like all monster trucks, it was made to be fast and strong.

You gripped the wheel. You could feel the vehicle's power. You decided you wanted to compete in a monster truck someday.

▲ There have been many versions of and drivers for Bigfoot since Bob Chandler created it in 1975.

Chapter 3

PUTTING IN TIME

Your desire to compete in a monster truck grew over the years. You got your driver's license when you were old enough. That allowed you to legally drive a monster truck.

But being a monster truck driver would take a lot of hard work. It would take months to get a truck ready to compete. Luckily your parents were friends with a group of **mechanics**. They knew a lot about machines and vehicles. They agreed to help you get a monster truck ready to race.

The monster truck took months to build. You started with the body of a large normal truck. This was a good option for first-time drivers. The mechanics helped you strip down the truck to its frame. They tore out everything so all that remained was a metal skeleton.

◀ Monster trucks are custom made. Each one is different.

They covered the frame in **fiberglass** panels and attached heavy-duty **shocks** and giant tires. Inside the cab, they designed controls that were perfect for you.

Each night after working on the truck, you went home to watch competition videos. You needed to know what to expect. The monster truck races you saw took place in huge arenas. Tons of dirt covered the floors.

The events have two parts. The first is rally racing. The dirt is shaped into two identical tracks. The tracks have tight turns and big ramps. Trucks race two at a time. The driver who finishes quickest moves on to the next round.

The other part of each monster truck event is freestyle action. This happens after the rally races. In freestyle, the drivers each take a turn on the dirt. They do cool tricks and spins. They also speed over ramps at high speeds to catch air.

After nearly a year, your truck was finally ready. It was time to train. You knew driving monster trucks could be dangerous. You needed to understand how the vehicle's weight shifted when you turned. You also needed to practice hitting ramps and flying through the air.

◀ **In rally races, drivers speed off ramps and fly above the ground.**

But before that, you had to check your safety gear. Your seat was not like a normal truck's seat. It curved up around your thighs when you sat in it. The back of the seat stretched straight up behind you. You could lean your head against it.

There was a **harness** instead of a regular seat belt. Its straps came down from above your shoulders. You wore a full-body suit, gloves, and a helmet. The helmet was to protect you in case you bounced around in the cab. The gloves were to help you grip the steering wheel.

You headed to an outdoor dirt track. Your ride started smoothly. But then there was a tight turn. You turned the wheel too tightly. The truck spun out. It took you weeks just to get the

THE SLAP WHEELIE

The first step in a slap wheelie is going off a ramp. Most ramps make the front end of the truck tilt up while in the air. But as the truck comes down, it starts to angle down. The front tires slap the ground first, making the front end bounce up. This is when the driver hits the gas. Doing this makes the truck tip onto the back wheels. It looks like it is standing straight up.

▲ **When a truck's front tires bounce up, drivers can hit the gas to do a slap wheelie.**

basics of driving the huge vehicle. Eventually, you started to get the hang of it.

Next, you practiced jumps. At first, it was scary speeding up the dirt ramps. But the only way to successfully navigate them was with lots of speed. You slowly learned how to stay in control as you hit bigger and bigger ramps.

Finally, it was time to learn a big trick: the slap **wheelie**. But you had only a few days before your first competition.

Chapter 4

GO TIME

It is time for your first monster truck rally race. You line up at the starting line. You are going against a driver in a bright red truck named Exploder.

A race official stands between the trucks. She has a green flag. She holds it over her head. You grip the wheel tighter. The big crowd screams louder. The official swoops the flag downward. You push down on the pedal. The tires grip the dirt. You are racing.

You get to the first hairpin turn. You think back to your training. You turn the wheel with perfect timing. Destructor drifts around the corner. Dirt flies up around you. There is no spinning out today. You gather speed into the straightaway.

Up ahead is a jump, followed by a line of four old, rusty cars. You hit the jump and fly over the first two. You land on top of the final two. They crumple under the weight of your monster truck.

◂ Big shocks attached to the wheels help pad the landing for the driver.

You fly around the final corner and gun it. You pass the finish line and look up on the arena's big screen.

"WINNER: DESTRUCTOR," it says. You have done it. You have achieved your dream.

You lose your next race to a monster called Chainbreaker. Chainbreaker ends up winning the entire rally event. Now it is time for your freestyle run.

You speed around and fly off some ramps. The crowd is loving it. Your freestyle time is almost up. You have time for only one last trick. You hit the ramp. For a moment, Destructor flies through the air. Then the front wheels slam down to the ground and bounce up again.

You hit the gas. The front end continues to rise. You feel the harness tighten on your shoulders to keep you in place. And then the front end stops rising. You are staring at the roof of the arena. You press the gas, and the truck starts to spin. The roof swirls above you. Your time is up. But the crowd is roaring as you show off your driving skills. You have made it as a monster truck driver.

◀ **Drivers who win events may get to compete in the Monster Jam World Finals each year.**

GLOSSARY

cab (kab): A cab is the front part of a truck where the steering wheel is located. You sit in the cab to drive your monster truck.

dashboard (DASH-bohrd): In the front of a normal car, the dashboard holds items such as the radio and different gauges. Monster trucks do not have a normal dashboard because they do not need them.

fiberglass (FYE-bur-glas): Fiberglass is a strong material made from fine glass fibers. The monster truck's fiberglass cab keeps you safe.

harness (HAHR-nis): A harness is a system of straps and buckles that tightens to keep something in place. The harness in your driver's seat keeps you from bouncing around while driving.

mechanics (muh-KAN-iks): Mechanics are people who repair machinery. Mechanics help you put the engine in your monster truck.

shocks (shahks): Shocks are devices attached to wheels that lessen the effects of bumps. Shocks soften your landing off big ramps.

wheelie (WEE-lee): A wheelie is when a truck rides on only the back tires. You perform a slap wheelie by bouncing the front tires off the ground and raising your truck onto the back two.

TO LEARN MORE

Books

Doolittle, Michael, and Susan E. Goodman. *Monster Trucks!* New York: Random House Publishing, 2010.

Gifford, Clive. *Fast and Furious: Monster Trucks*. New York: Octopus Publishing, 2014.

Kane, Tim. *Monster Mega Trucks . . . and Other Four-Wheeled Creatures*. Chicago: Triumph Books, 2014.

Web Sites

Visit our Web site for links about monster trucks: childsworld.com/links

Note to Parents, Teachers, and Librarians: We routinely verify our Web links to make sure they are safe and active sites. So encourage your readers to check them out!

SELECTED BIBLIOGRAPHY

Borrelli, Christopher. "13 Things You Don't Know about the Origins of the First Monster Truck." *Chicago Tribune*. Chicago Tribune, 12 Mar. 2010. Web. 10 Jun. 2015.

Leahy, Joseph. "King Kong out to Crush Bigfoot's Claim to Fame as First Monster Truck." *NPR News*. National Public Radio, 27 Dec. 2014. Web. 3 Jun. 2015.

Monster Truck Racing Association. "International Safety Rules Version 24.1." *Monster Truck Racing Association*. MTRA International, 2014. Web. 10 Jun. 2015.

INDEX

arena, 5, 7, 15, 21

Bigfoot, 10

cab, 10–11, 15, 16
Chainbreaker, 21
Chandler, Bob, 10
Crusher, 10, 11

Destructor, 5, 7, 19, 21

frame, 13, 15
freestyle, 15, 21

mechanic, 13
Monster Truck Racing Association, 9

rally race, 15, 19, 21
ramps, 15, 16, 17, 21

safety, 9–10, 16,
shocks, 15
size, 9–10
slap wheelie, 16, 17

track, 7, 15, 16

ABOUT THE AUTHOR

Alex Monnig is a freelance journalist from Saint Louis, Missouri, who now lives in Sydney, Australia. He graduated with his master's degree from the University of Missouri in 2010. During his career, he has spent time covering sporting events around the world.